D1458535

Books by Paul Howard

Bugville
Trouble in Bugville

'Madcap and fun.' *We Love This Book*

'A fast-moving tale of heroic heroes
and villainous villains, packed with
cliff-hanging action.' *Booktrust*

'This book is very funny and has a big
slug in it who burps and shoots sparks
from his tentacles.' James, 10

and now it's
time for

BIRR
23 NOV 2021
WITHDRAWN

TROUBLE IN
BUGVILLE

Written and illustrated
by Paul Howard

EGMONT

EGMONT

For my bug-loving friend,
Fiona Mellon-Grant.

Trouble in Bugville first published in Great Britain 2013
by Egmont UK Limited
The Yellow Building. 1 Nicholas Road
London W11 4AN

Text and illustrations copyright © 2013 Paul Howard

The moral rights of the author have been asserted

ISBN 978 1 4052 6472 3

1 3 5 7 9 10 8 6 4 2

www.egmont.co.uk

A CIP catalogue record for this title is available
from the British Library

Printed and bound in Great Britain by the CPI Group

46865/1

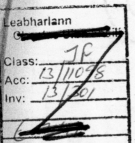

EGMONT

Our story began over a century ago, when seventeen-year-old
Egmont Harald Petersen found a coin in the street. He was on
his way to buy a flyswatter, a small hand-operated printing
machine that he then set up in his tiny apartment.

The coin brought him such good luck that today Egmont has
offices in over 30 countries around the world. And that lucky
coin is still kept at the company's head offices in Denmark.

CONTENTS

This is Bugville.

One super cool city.

Dozens of parks and ice rinks.

Scores of stores and libraries.

Hundreds of concert halls.

Thousands of lice-cream parlours.

And millions of . . .

BUGS!

Bugs like these: an extraordinary housefly and a brave, tiny midge – Superfly and, er, Midge! Bugville's favourite home-grown heroes. Everybody loves these flies!

Never ones to brag or boast, Superfly and Midge had certainly made Bugville a safer city, dropping dozens of beastly bugs behind bars. OK, so there were still a couple of rotten bugs causing havoc out there, like . . .

. . . the dirty dung beetle rolling down Froghopper Avenue on a giant ball of dung, threatening to splat everything in sight!

Chapter 1

DUNGER!

Superfly and Midge were already in action. blazing through the air after the dung beetle.

'Kick into top speed, Midge,' yelled Superfly. 'We gotta make Slime Square before that dung ball!'

The dung beetle was on his ball, hurtling down the street, bouncing off buildings and crushing parked cars. If his dung ball reached Slime Square, hundreds

of innocent bugs would be squashed –
FLAT!

Superfly and Midge shot past the beetle and landed further down the street. Terriflied bugs were fleeing for their lives, leaving Superfly and Midge to face the looming ball of dung alone.

CLANG! The dung ball crushed a bus stop.

SpLAT! The dung ball floored a news-stand.

GULP! Bugville's heroes were next!

Superfly stretched his arms out to stop the speeding ball.

Midge took a piece of gum from his belt-pouch and flicked it into his mouth.

But wait! That wasn't any old gum. It was SUPER gum, guaranteed to blow big, bouncy bubbles!

As the dung ball raced towards them like a giant bowling ball, Superfly screwed his eyes shut. Midge chomped his gum and . . . blew a bubble!

Then, just as the giant ball of dung was about to splatter them . . .

SPLAZOOOO

. . . it spun off into the sky!

Midge had blown a SUPER bubble and bounced that dung beetle – and his ball – up, up, up into the air. What a clever midge!

SPLASH! The dung ball fell into the river, soaking several water-striders, and floated out to sea.

oom!

SMASH! The beetle crushed a neon sign, before running off across the rooftops.

Midge popped more gum into his mouth and chewed. What was he going to do now?

On Superfly's signal – **_SCHLOP!_** – Midge spat a big blob of sticky gum at the beetle's feet. Yuck!

The gum stuck and stretched as the beetle tried to get away. Then, with one foot in the air, he froze. The gum had hardened.

'Well, well. If it isn't the most dung-headed beetle in Bugville,' said Superfly, seeing the villain up close. 'Duncan Donut. Gum his hands together, Midge – we're taking him down.'

The heroes prised Duncan Donut from the roof, lifted him down and handed him over to the police.

Superfly and Midge. The city's favourite heroes. They'd saved Bugville – *again*.

Moments later, the boys were surrounded by news reporters, all asking questions:

Superfly, how did you make that huge bubble appear from nowhere?

Superfly, how did you shoot gum from your fingers?

Superfly, who's your favourite pop stinger?

Ah, poor Midge. They never asked him anything!

Never mind, Superfly wasn't going to answer them anyway. He'd already turned to face the crowds. Everyone in Bugville was waiting for Superfly to shout three words. Three words he always said. Three little words that let them know Bugville was safe once more.

'PIECE 'O CAKE!'

And then – **FIZZz!** – Bugville's craziest ever – **WHIZZ!** – street carnival – **WHEEEEEEEE!** – began.

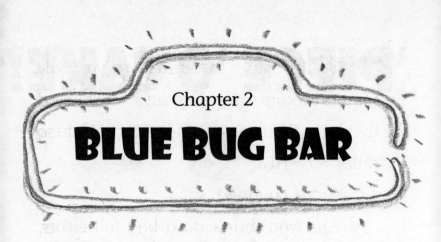

Chapter 2

BLUE BUG BAR

Cheers ran out from the Blue Bug Bar as
Superfly and Midge dropped in for a quick
bite to eat.

Woo-hoo!

Let's hear it!
Come on!

'Well, I have to hand it to ya,' said Mama Buitoni, stepping out from behind the bar. 'You sure snagged that dung roller, Superfly.'

Midge coughed.

'And you didn't do a bad job either, cutie-fly,' the busy bar-bee added, smoothing her apron. 'You boys've really turned Bugville round. Now, what d'ya wanna eat? It's on the house, flies.'

Hey Mama, turn the TV up! Bugville Smash is on.

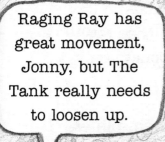

'Aw, that Tank dude sucks, man,' a weevil blurted.

'Raging Ray'll run rings around him, anyways,' a wasp added. 'He's a supersonic sawfly!'

Mama Buitoni lifted their plates. 'I dunno, flies,' she said. 'That Goliath beetle looks hard to beat.'

'SSSSSH!' the weevil hissed. 'It's back on!'

Everyone booed as The Tank hit Raging Ray with a Bell Slap – **WHAM!**

– power-slammed him with a Fore-leg Smash – **POW!** – floored him with a Super-kick – **WHACK!** – finished him with a Big Splash – **BAM!** – and then gave him a Stink Face – **POO!**

Poor Raging Ray – a Stink Face! How humiliating!

The Tank had won easily. But everyone started to boo – in the audience and in the Blue Bug Bar too.

'Shut up already!' yelled the wasp. 'I wanna hear what Lacey Russell has to say!'

'That pond-skater's right, man,' the weevil said. 'My grandma's got more zip!'

Superfly's antennae vibrated. His phone was ringing. 'Excuse me, flies,' he said, lifting the phone off his weapons belt.

An old grasshopper appeared on the mini-screen.

Midge sighed. It was Grand Master Grasshopper. Although he had been blinded in a terrible pillow fight, Grand Master could still see – see the future, that is. Unfortunately, what he saw was usually grim.

'I've had a terrible vision, young

one,' the grasshopper began. 'About your future.'

'Really?' Superfly said, staring at the mini-screen with interest. But just as the grasshopper was about to reply – something smashed through the old bug's apartment door.

'Grand Master!' Superfly cried as his tutor dropped his phone and disappeared from view.

SMASH! BASH! CHOP!

Superfly could hear the door being smashed to pieces. Then, suddenly – **FIZZZZz** – the mini-screen went fuzzy.

Oh my! Superfly and Midge had to get to Tick Towers and save the old grasshopper – **FAST!**

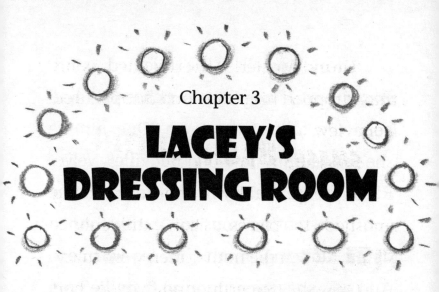

Chapter 3
LACEY'S DRESSING ROOM

Over at the TV studios, Bugville Smash had finished and the judges had gone backstage.

Stag Taggart was watching a replay of the semi-final. Freya Lemar was on the phone. And Lacey Russell was sipping tea in her dressing room.

Lacey Russell – the talented pond-skater – why, her rags to riches tale had been the talk of the town. One minute she was skimming along Bugville's Velvet River, the next she was the star of Flame – an ice-skating musical extravaganza about dancing moths in leg-warmers. And now she was a judge on Bugville's top TV show!

As the long-legged beauty was arranging some flowers in a vase, the door flew open and an earwig barged in.

Lacey stared at the short, round bug as he scanned the room from behind his dark glasses. She recognised him from the studio – he was The Tank's manager. He clicked his huge pincers and spoke.

'I didn't like those bad things you said about my boy, Tankie, Missy Russell.'

'Oh, really?' Lacey began. But then she stopped. The cheeky earwig had picked up her vase of flowers!

'You should be sayin' NICE things about Tankie,' he grumbled, putting the vase down in front of the mirror.

'Listen, Mr . . . ?'

'Wig. The name's Wig.'

'Well, Mr Wig, The Tank's moves are mechanical,' Lacey insisted. 'And besides,' she went on, 'you can't stop me saying what I think.'

'Oh,' Mr Wig chortled, 'but I CAN.' He whipped off his dark glasses, revealing two huge, spinning eyes. 'Whether you like it . . . or NOT!'

Round and round his big eyes swirled, capturing Lacey's gaze. Whirling circles, spinning and spinning . . . Why, Mr Wig was a hypno . . . hypno . . . HYPNOTIST!

And he'd hypnotised Lacey Russell!

The bad bug slid his glasses back over his eyes. 'Well now, Missy Russell,' he said. 'Are you ready to make Tankie the biggest hero Bugville's ever seen?'

He lifted Lacey's ice skates and dangled them in front of her nodding head. 'Good,' he sighed. 'Then get yo' skates on!'

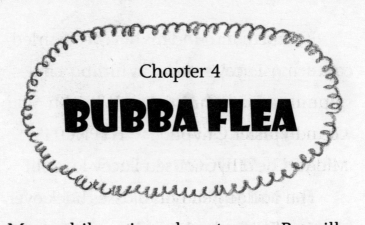

Chapter 4

BUBBA FLEA

Meanwhile, in downtown Bugville, Superfly and Midge blazed through the night sky. Grand Master Grasshopper was in trouble – there was no time to lose!

Midge tore on to the balcony of the grasshopper's 81st-floor apartment and tumbled behind a potted plant.

Superfly landed on the wall above.

'What can
you see, Midge?'
Superfly called. 'Is
Grand Master OK?
Midge? . . . MIDGE?'

But Midge had gone.

He'd already slipped through an air vent and disappeared inside.

Superfly peered through the glass door. There was no sign of Grand Master. And no sign of . . . Wait! There was Midge – flying up to let him in.

'Thanks, buddy,' whispered Superfly, climbing inside.

'Ah, young one,' said a welcoming

voice from the next room. 'We've been waiting for you.'

'Grand Master!' called Superfly, as he flew next door. 'You're alive!'

'Apparently so,' the old grasshopper said, checking his pulse.

'But we thought . . .'

'Ssssh,' his ancient tutor interrupted. 'We are in the presence of a supreme being . . .' He stood aside to reveal a hunched figure, cradling a sitar. 'BUBBA FLEA!'

Superfly and Midge stared at the bubble-haired flea on the sofa. Was this the legendary bug that Grand Master

had often spoken about? His dearest friend, who had once been the most famous wrestler in Bugville, Mystifly, before catastrophe struck and he caught chronic catarrh, forcing him to hang up his costume forever?

Bubba Flea – why, Grand Master had been telling them tales about him since they were maggots in Bluey Bottle's Circus.

'Pleased to meet you, oh Great One,' Superfly said, bowing to the wrinkly cat-flea. 'We've heard so much about you.'

Bubba Flea nodded in reply.

'We thought Grand Master was in trouble,' Superfly continued. 'We saw someone breaking his door down!'

'As I told you, young one, I am perfectly well,' Grand Master said. 'As for that . . .' He pointed at the remains of the apartment door. 'Bubba never knocks on doors, he chops them down – bare handed!'

Superfly glanced at the fragile-looking cat-flea and gulped.

'Bubba Flea has come to share his ancient teachings with you,' the old grasshopper announced. 'To prepare you for what terror is to come.'

Suddenly, Bubba Flea plucked his sitar . . .

PINGY, PONGY. PING, PING, PING. PIIIING!

'Ah,' said Grand Master. 'Bubba is ready!'

The mystical cat-flea nodded, set down his instrument and declared: 'Now is time to WORK!'

Five awful hours passed. Five hours spent doing yoga poses like this:

And this:

And, worst of all, this:

Followed by an hour of 'chops' . . .

. . . before, finally, Bubba Flea finished them off with an intense massage.

No wonder the boys fell into a deep sleep afterwards. Superfly and Midge were well and truly – what's the word? – pooped.

Chapter 5
CRIME-STOPPERS

Already well-known as Bugville's favourite news reporter, appearing on Bugville Smash had made Freya Lemar a big celebrity. She'd been busy doing photo shoots, school visits, charity lunches, radio shows, library talks, napkin-folding demonstrations . . . Why, she'd hardly stopped to eat! So, at the first opportunity, her hornet workmate, Melba Modem, took her for brunch.

'So, what about that gorgeous Goliath beetle on your show, honey?' Melba asked as they headed downtown.

'You mean The Tank?'

'Mmm-hmm, that's him . . .' Melba checked her lipstick in a compact mirror. 'Is he, er, dating anyone?'

'Seriously?' questioned Freya.

'Absolutely!'

Freya threw her hand over Melba's mouth.

'SSSSHH! Look!'

There, at the end of an alleyway, a slender, masked figure was cutting a hole in a jeweller's shop window – with an ice-skate! She was about to climb through when . . .

FLASH!

Freya's camera-flash went off as she took a photo.

The thief looked over, but then disappeared through the hole.

'Oh my stars,' Freya gasped. 'Melba! Are you thinking what I'm thinking?'

'What? She's got amazing legs?'

'No!' Freya scowled. 'Her eyes! There was something strange about her eyes.'

'Really?' Melba replied, lifting her phone. 'I only noticed her legs.'

'Who're you calling?'

'The cops,' Melba answered.

'But Superfly and Midge'll be on their way . . . QUICK!' Freya suddenly cried, shoving her friend behind a waste bin. 'She's coming back!'

A long leg poked out of the window.

'My phone!' shrieked Melba, as it dropped through a grating.

'Never mind that,' said Freya. 'LOOK!'

There, held in the thief's clutches, was the largest, sparkliest jewel in Bugville – **BLING!** – the Daddy Diamond!

Suddenly, a huge silhouette filled the end of the alley.

'What's The Tank doing here?' Freya asked. But Melba couldn't answer. She was too love-struck to talk.

The Tank grabbed the jewel thief and pulled the precious diamond from her grasp.

'Oh, where are Superfly and Midge?' Freya asked, searching the sky.

'Still in bed probably,' Melba said dryly. 'Looks like the job's already done now anyhow.'

It was true. The Tank held the wriggly

thief in one hand and the priceless diamond in the other. But, with no trustworthy bug there to mind the diamond, and no police to take the thief, The Tank had to let one go . . .

'Look at that,' sighed Melba as the long-legged thief picked herself up and scampered away across the rooftops. 'That's SO romantic.'

Freya rolled her eyes. 'Come on, Melba,' she said, taking her friend's arm. 'The show's over.'

The girls moved on to Mothburger Square, where the police had arrived to return the Daddy Diamond. 'Superfly and Midge have probably caught that thief by now too,' Freya said.

'Honey, you gotta face facts,' Melba snapped. 'Superfly and Midge ain't up to the job any more. See that gorgeous hunk o' love?' She pointed at The Tank. 'He's the

C'mon everybody. Get your picture taken with Bugville's superhero!

only hero round here right now!'

Meanwhile, on the other side of the square, Superfly and Midge had finally arrived. Not that anyone had noticed – everyone wanted to see THE TANK!

News reporters and TV crews swarmed around the new hero as Mr Wig appeared at his side.

'So everybody gets their picture with Tankie, *I'll* be takin' questions. But firs', lemme say how proud I am o' my boy here.' The crowd cheered. 'Also, I wanna remind y'all to watch the final of *Bugville Smash* tonight to see Tankie WIN!'

The crowd erupted. Then, the

earwig threw his arms up in the air and disappeared into a sea of bobbing microphones.

Superfly and Midge watched from a distance. Usually, *they* were surrounded by crowds and reporters. Usually, everyone wanted *their* photograph. Usually, *Superfly and Midge* had saved the day. But not today.

Superfly felt bad. He and Midge had been so tired after training with Bubba Flea that they'd slept through the emergency call on Superfly's antennae.

Stood away from the hubbub, Superfly spotted Freya Lamar waiting for Melba to get her photo taken with The Tank.

'Where were you?' she called.

Superfly hung his head. He felt such a failure. But at that moment, his antennae vibrated.

'Bubba Flea wants to see you, young one,' Grand Master Grasshopper said. 'NOW!' **GULP!**

Chapter 6

BUBBA'S WAY OF SEEING

In Grand Master's apartment, Bubba Flea stared at his new students.

'Why so glum?' he asked. 'What happen? Tell Bubba.'

'We were too late to catch a jewel thief, Great One,' Superfly confessed. 'The Daddy Diamond was saved by a TV-show contestant called The Tank.'

Midge's top lip curled at the mention of The Tank's name.

'Sorry,' sighed Superfly. 'We failed.'

The mystical cat-flea closed his eyes.

'In that case,' he sighed, 'Bubba must teach you lesson.'

Superfly and Midge glanced at each other nervously. What terrible punishment was Bubba Flea going to give them? Walking on hot coals? Eating Brussels sprouts? Listening to him playing his sitar?

Midge's teeth chattered. Superfly's antennae shook. Together, they watched as Bubba Flea's face turned purple. They huddled closer as his expression turned fierce. They trembled as Bubba raised his back leg. Then . . .

Pwwwwwwwwwwwwwrrrrrrrttttttttttt!

Bubba Flea let out a rotten, stinky fart.

Superfly coughed as the cat-flea's pong filled the room.

Oh no, he thought, *he's going to gas us!*

Midge clasped his throat, just as Grand Master Grasshopper burst in with a can of air freshener.

'Pardon me . . .' Bubba Flea said. 'Bubba's bottom has removed wind, making Bubba happy. In same way, your mind must remove bad feeling and make you happy.'

The choking heroes looked confused, so Grand Master explained further. 'He means that you should not punish yourself over one mistake, young one,' he gasped, spraying freshener around the room. 'Let it go and move on. And remember – no hero can stop *every* crime – not even you.'

Superfly and Midge sighed with relief. Like their minds, the air cleared and, at last, Bubba Flea opened his eyes.

'Enough,' he said. 'Watch Bubba.'

He pulled two yoga mats from his robe and laid them out on the floor. Superfly's heart sank. Oh no! Not more yoga!

'This,' Bubba Flea told them, raising his legs up over his head, 'is the KING of all yoga poses.' He moved into a perfect headstand, then slowly returned to rest. 'Now,' he said. 'You try.'

Seventeen attempts later, Superfly had mastered the headstand.

'How do we look now, chap?' asked Bubba Flea.

'Er . . .' Superfly panted. 'Different.'

'Correct,' Bubba smiled. 'The headstand make us see everything – and everyone – in different way. Now, practice!'

Superfly and Midge spent two hours practicing headstands. When they had finished, the heroes found Bubba Flea in the next room, laughing at old episodes of *Bugville Smash*.

Superfly coughed. 'Excuse us, oh Great One, but what's so funny?'

'Oh, chap!' Bubba Flea chuckled. 'This Tank tears them all apart, believe Bubba!'

Superfly's shoulders sagged. Was Bubba Flea really that impressed with The Tank?

Midge hissed at the screen.

'Midge!' Superfly snapped.

'No, no – little chappie's right to hiss,' the old flea said. 'This Tank – he look like hero on outside, but inside he is empty.'

Bubba Flea pressed the pause button. 'This Tank,' he said, 'has no . . . VIBE.' Midge landed on The Tank's frozen image on the TV screen. Then he turned upside-down and snarled.

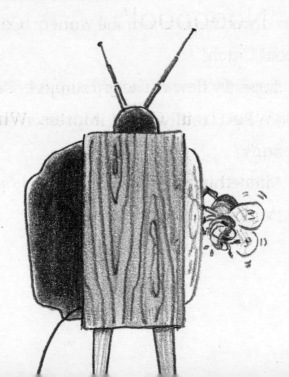

'You learn quick, little chappie,' Bubba
Flea said. 'To see clearly, we must look from
all angles!'

But before he could explain further . . .

CRASH! CLING! CLONG!

. . . they were interrupted. It was
Grand Master. He was having another
vision.

'**Noooooo!**' he wailed. 'Catch!
Catch! Catch!'

Superfly flew to the grasshopper's aid.

'What is it, Grand Master. What's
wrong?'

'Something . . . terrible!' the grasshopper
wheezed.

'Where, Grand Master?'

'Sliiiiime Square!' he cried, gripping Superfly's costume.

'When, Master?'

'When?' the old bug repeated, *'NOW!'*

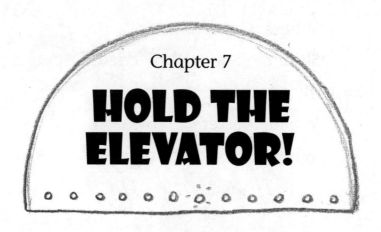

Chapter 7

HOLD THE ELEVATOR!

Slime Square was at the heart of Bugville's theatre-land. But when Superfly and Midge got there, there was only one place to see a show – the Fly Star Building!

The glass elevator on the outside of the skyscraper was hanging dangerously above the ground. Some nimble, masked

villain had cut its cables, using the blade of . . . an ice-skate!

It was the long-legged jewel thief! Again!

Crouched on top of the elevator, she was just about to cut the last cable, when Superfly arrived.

Inside the elevator was Sister Aphid and her class of screaming aphids.

'You're not getting away with it this time, lady-long-legs!' Superfly shouted.

But the thief pulled something from her pocket and hurled it at Superfly. It was . . .

. . . a STINK BOMB!

POO!

Midge pulled a mask over his nose, ready to chase after the bomb-dropping villain.

But he couldn't –
Superfly had been hit
by the smelly blast and
was tumbling towards
the ground!

Midge kicked his
turbo boots into super-
speed and zipped down
through the stink cloud.

His mouth rippled.

His eyes streamed.

His tiny heart
pounded.

Boom . . . *boom* . . .

BOOM!

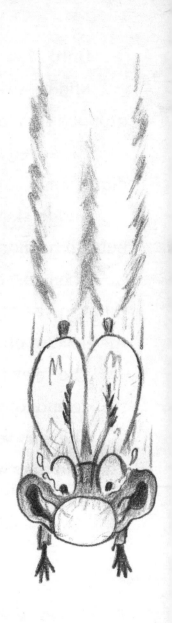

Until . . .

Midge swept his partner up and dropped him in the fresh air.

He waved smelling salts, but Superfly didn't stir.

Midge slapped him round the face, but still he didn't wake.

Then, just as Midge was about to give him the kiss of life, the last cable holding the elevator above them . . . snapped!

The elevator hurtled through the stink cloud towards the ground!

The loud screams woke Superfly.

And they were getting closer – FAST!

Superfly sprang up to catch the falling elevator. But suddenly he froze. A hulking silhouette was stomping through the stink cloud.

'What is *that?*' asked Superfly, using his anti-fog vision to take a closer look. 'Oh no,' he murmured. 'It's The Tank!'

Midge spat splinters through his teeth, as the diamond-saving hero caught the elevator in mid-air, carried it out of the stink cloud and set it down safely.

Cheering fans rushed to the Goliath beetle's side. He'd saved the Daddy Diamond and now he'd saved Sister Aphid and her class! Stink gas didn't bother him, no wrestler could beat him and he could pose for fans for hours! Why, The Tank was the perfect hero!

Bless you, Mr Tank.

Crowds stampeded and news reporters surrounded The Tank as Sister Aphid and her young aphids were led to safety.

Mr Wig appeared. 'OK, everybody!' he shouted into a snatched microphone. 'I jus' wanna say a few words.'

The noisy crowd settled down.

'T'day, my boy Tankie's recovered the Daddy Diamond . . . and saved Sister Aphid and her class!'

The crowd cheered loudly.

'Also,' he continued, gesturing for calm. 'After he's won Bugville Smash tonight, my boy's gonna be the greatest hero Bugville's ever seen!'

The crowd went wild!

But Mr Wig hadn't finished. 'One mo' thing!' he bellowed. 'Bugville can rely on Tankie. He won't let this city down . . . not like Superfly and Midge!'

The crowd roared with laughter.

Superfly felt sick.

'Maybe that earwig's right, Midge,' he mumbled. 'Maybe I'm not a hero any more.'

Poor Superfly. He'd forgotten Bubba's

lesson and forgotten who he was. But, luckily, someone knew.

'Hey!' a little bed bug gurgled. 'You're Superfly! You're the best!'

'Thanks, kid,' Superfly said, half-smiling. 'But I don't think –'

'Say "Piece o' Cake!" Say "Piece o' Cake!"' the bouncing bed bug repeated, pulling on his idol's suit.

'Sorry, kid, but –'

'Pleeeeeeeaaaase!' the little bug begged.

Superfly looked over at The Tank and Mr Wig and sighed. 'I can't,' he said. 'Not yet.'

Chapter 8
TWO BEAUTIES

After the morning they'd had, Freya Lemar and Melba Modem deserved to be pampered at Belle's Beauty Bar. There,

they could join other lady bugs and enjoy relaxing wing rubs and foot massages. They could stroll wig-less and wear paper pants without a care in the world.

Freya Lemar – legs waxed, nails done, wings sprayed – was smothered in steaming-hot towels, enjoying a seaweed body wrap in peace and quiet.

Oh, hang on. Quiet? With Melba around?

'Well, anyways, I told him – ladies don't do that kinda thing. Hey! What about The Tank, honey. Can I meet him again after the show tonight?'

'Sure,' Freya sighed.

'Ooo-wee!' Melba cooed, splashing her feet around in a tank of tiny fish. 'He's such a hero. Where's he from anyways, honey?'

'Phew! I'm not sure,' Freya panted through her hot towel. 'Isn't this all a little tough on Superfly?'

'Superfly?' Melba scoffed. 'Honey, I

told ya, he's old news!' She picked up a TV remote. 'Speakin' of news, mind if I turn on the TV? I wanna see if the hunky Tank's on.'

'Oh, Melba. I can't believe Rose Baumer said that!' Freya cried.

'I know!' Melba said. 'She'd better not get near my gorgeous Tank. Cheeky . . .'

'No, I meant what she said about it being the end for Superfly and Midge!'

'Well,' Melba sighed. 'I keep tellin' ya, they're old news, honey.'

A beauty therapist came in to unwrap Freya.

'Ugh!' cried Melba. 'You smell like a fish market!'

As Freya showered, moisturised and got dressed, she wondered how The Tank always arrived on the scene at the right moment.

Just then, her phone rang.

82

83

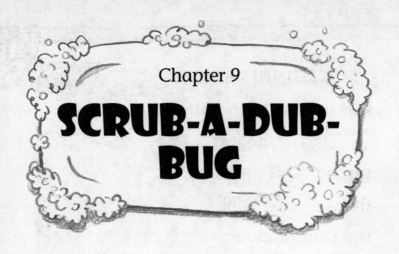

Chapter 9
SCRUB-A-DUB-BUG

Across town, outside a docklands apartment, a phone line was swinging. It had been cut by the blade . . . of an ice-skate!

Inside, a superstar wrestler was taking a shower. He sang and whistled, scrubbed and rinsed, and then . . . he dropped his soapy sponge.

SSSSHHH! Someone was in his bathroom!

Stag Taggart turned off the shower. Someone was coming closer!

Stag Taggart grabbed a towel. Someone pulled back the curtain!

'W - w - what are you doin' here?' the wrestler stammered.

'We're meant to be meetin' at the Waterfront.'

Stag Taggart was confused. What was Lacey Russell doing in his bathroom? How did she get into his apartment? Why was she wearing ice-skates? And why were her eyes so glassy?

But before he could ask her any questions, Lacey spun round and left the room. 'Follow me,' she demanded. 'There are too many mirrors in here.'

With a towel firmly wrapped around his waist, Stag Taggart followed her into the lounge.

Waiting there was an earwig.

'Hey, what is this?' Stag Taggart asked. 'What's goin' on?'

The earwig spun round to face him.

'Mr Wig?'

'That's right,' the earwig smirked.

'Oh, I get it,' Stag said. 'You know that I found out about The Tank's little secret . . .'

Mr Wig lowered his dark glasses.

'And that I'm gonna tell everyone on Bugville Smash . . . TONIGHT!'

The earwig's eyes began to swirl.

'So you've come to stop me,' Stag continued, flexing his beefy arm muscles. 'Well, let's see you try.'

Mr Wig whipped off his glasses. Round and round his huge eyes spun, seizing Stag's gaze . . . whirling and twirling . . . shrinking in circles . . . deeper and deeper . . . until Stag Taggart had been hypnotised!

'You won't be revealin' any of Tankie's secrets now, Staggy,' Mr Wig said.

Stag Taggart stared blankly ahead.

'You gonna tell ev'rybody he's gonna be the biggest superhero Bugville's ever seen!'

Mr Wig popped his glasses back on.

'Now go put some clothes on,' he said. 'We can't get Freya Lemar with you naked like that!'

Chapter 10
WAITING

It was late afternoon and in a few hours' time Bugville's most popular TV show would begin. On school runs and coffee breaks, everyone was talking about Bugville Smash.

Everyone except Superfly and Midge.

The two heroes were sitting by the river, thinking about their dreadful day.

'I still don't get it, Midge,' Superfly

said. 'How did The Tank breathe in that stink cloud?'

Midge curled his lip.

'How come he's there whenever any trouble starts?'

Midge gnashed his teeth.

'And who was that masked villain?'

Midge gasped.

'Who?'

But Midge hadn't worked out who the villain was – he'd spotted someone.

TWANG!

Midge flicked Superfly's antennae. There, leaning against the embankment wall, was a beautiful blue-bottle.

'Hey, Freya,' Superfly called.

'Oh,' the startled beauty cried. 'Superfly! Hi. How's it going?'

Superfly leant beside her. 'Well,' he sniffed. 'We've had better days.'

Midge landed between them and licked his teeth.

'So, where were you flies earlier at the jewellers and Slime Square?' Freya asked.

Midge preened his eyebrows and coughed.

'Oh, sorry, Midge!' Freya smiled. 'I

didn't see you there. How are you?'

Midge blew her a kiss and flew back on to Superfly's head.

'Oh, Midge,' Freya blushed, completely forgetting her question. 'You're so adorable.'

A river-boat passed by.

'Where have Stag and Lacey got to?' Freya said, looking at her watch. 'They're never normally this late.'

Freya leaned towards Superfly. 'Stag has something to tell us,' she whispered. 'Something he couldn't say over the phone.'

'Oh, really?' Superfly said, raising an antenna.

'Something about . . . The Tank!'
Midge snarled.

'There is something fishy about him, isn't there?' Freya said. 'The way he turns up at every crime scene, just in time.'

Midge impersonated a phone ringing.

'You're right, Midge,' Freya said. 'I'll call Stag now.' She pulled out her phone and dialled a number, but . . . 'That's strange!' she said. 'Stag's mobile's dead too. Just like his home phone was earlier.'

'We'll check it out,' Superfly assured her. 'Come on, Midge.'

'Thanks, flies. I hope he's OK,' she said, checking her watch again. 'Look, I need to go and get ready for the show. Call me about Stag, won't you?'

As Freya ran off, Superfly's antennae vibrated – his own phone was ringing.

'Come quick, young one,' Grand Master said from the mini-screen. 'Bubba

Flea is leaving and has a gift for you.'

'A gift?' asked Superfly. 'What is it, Grand Master?'

'Well, it's a present usually given on special occasions, like birthdays, but that's not the point. Bubba's gift will save your lives!'

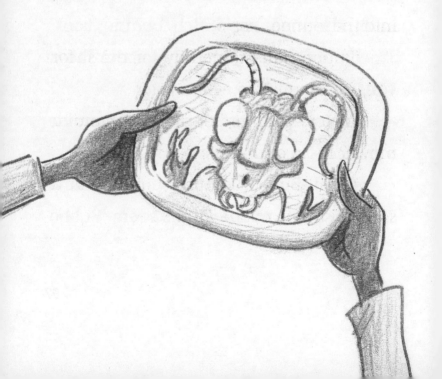

Chapter 11

BUBBA'S GIFT

As soon as Superfly and Midge arrived back at Tick Towers, Bubba Flea led them into the lounge.

'Bubba has something special for you,' he promised.

What could it be? Popcorn and a movie? Pizza and fizzy pop? No . . .

'This!' Bubba beamed, pointing at a sand pit in the middle of the room.

'Now, take off weapon belt and clothes and put these loin-cloth on,' Bubba Flea said, waving two old rags at them.

Midge held out his loin-cloth and squirmed.

'Loin-cloth is worn like a nappy, chappie,' Bubba explained to the horriflied midge. 'Now, chop, chop! It is time to wrestle!'

Putting on their loin-cloths, Superfly and Midge stepped into the sand pit.

'Now,' Bubba Flea said. 'Wrestle!'

Superfly tried not to laugh, as he made a half-hearted grab for Midge. But the midge was too fast. He zipped down and flipped his partner off his feet. THUMP! 'Hey!' Superfly grumbled, jumping back up. Midge grabbed him by the nose and rocked his head from side to side. Superfly went to flick Midge off, but the nippy bug had already zoomed down and flipped him again.

THUD!

'Ow!' Superfly yelped. It was no good. He would have to play dirty to win. He grabbed two handfuls of sand and got up.

Midge darted around him.

'Ha!' said Superfly, throwing sand at his pal. 'Take that!'

Midge spat sand out from his teeth,

dived down and grabbed two handfuls of his own. But before he could throw them . . .

Bubba Flea raised his arms. 'Enough!'

Superfly and Midge dropped the sand and gulped. Were they about to be punished?

The mystical cat-flea closed his eyes and smiled. 'Bubba is happy. You see, sometime unexpected thing is more use than any weapon on your belt.'

Superfly and Midge were confused.

'He means that, without your usual weapons, young one,' Grand Master explained, 'you were forced to fight using the sand.'

Superfly grinned. Wow! He'd actually done something right.

'That is it!' Bubba Flea suddenly clapped. 'Bubba's work is done. All that left to do is give you gift.'

The ancient guru searched through

his robes. 'Won't be tick . . .' he said. 'It here somewhere . . .'

He dug into the robe's deepest fold and pulled out . . . a bag!

Superfly looked at Midge. A bag? How would that save their lives? Surely there was some mistake?

'Do not question the gift,' the wrinkly grasshopper declared. 'Treat it with respect. It will help save you, and Bugville.'

'Take it!' Bubba ordered.

'B-b-but . . . isn't this your wash-bag, Great One?' Superfly stammered, looking at the toothbrush and hairspray poking out.

Bubba Flea opened his eyes and swapped the wash-bag with another bag from his robe.

'You see,' he said. 'Everyone make mistake sometime – even Bubba.'

'Thank you, Great One.' Superfly bowed. Midge started to unzip the bag . . .

'NO!' Bubba cried. 'Do not open bag!

It is not time to use what is inside.'

'Oh,' Superfly said, plucking Midge off the zip. 'But how will we know when the time is right, Great One?'

'You will know . . . from within,' the cat-flea said, pumping a fist to his chest. 'Believe Bubba.'

The mystical flea threw his sitar on his back and checked the time. 'Holy Moly,' he cried. 'I must go! Fleasyjet won't wait!'

Grand Master raised an antenna at Superfly and coughed.

'Oh,' the hero said. 'Thank you, oh Great One. For all you have taught us.'

'Enough!' Bubba Flea said. 'Thank

Grand Master. But remember – believe
Bubba.'

And with that, the mystical cat-flea
jumped off the balcony.

The room fell silent.

'Bubba Flea,' Grand Master sighed,

'has flown.'

Then, like magic, a gentle breeze from the balcony delivered a note. A last message that read:

To be a true hero, remember:

PEE-PEE

Put heart and soul in
every fight.

Every crime cannot be stopped.

Expect to make mistakes but
be sure to let them go.

Perfect weapon is not always
on your belt.

Everyone must be looked
at in all ways to see truth.

Enough!

Believe Bubba

Chapter 12
THE CHAUFFEUR

It was almost time for the live final of Bugville Smash and Freya Lemar was just about ready. Still concerned about Stag Taggart, she quickly checked her phone for any messages. But there was nothing, until . . .

BBBBBRRRRRIIIINNNGGGGGG!!!!!

. . . her phone rang.

110

Freya Lemar was so excited to be in a limo. So excited, she forgot to ask Stag where he'd been or why both his phones were dead. So excited, she didn't notice that neither Stag nor Lacey were moving.

But once her excitement faded, she began to ask questions: 'So where were you earlier, Lacey? You never said.'

But the ice-skating star didn't answer.

'What about you, Stag? You didn't make it to the Waterfront.'

The wrestling champ looked straight ahead.

'And what's up with your phones?'

Stag didn't even blink.

'And what did you want to tell us, anyway?'

But before Freya could ask why they were ignoring her, the car suddenly turned into a dark back alley, flinging the passengers sideways.

'Hey, driver,' Freya called from the back seat. 'What's going on? Where you taking us?'

The chauffeur slammed on the brakes, flinging her forward.

'You ask a lot of questions, Miss Lemar,' he said in a deep, syrupy voice. 'Too many questions,' he added, turning round.

'Oh, my!' Freya cried. 'Mr Wig! Why are you driving us to the studios? Couldn't the studio book a real chauffeur?'

Mr Wig took off his dark glasses.

'And why've we stopped in this dark, smelly alleyway?'

'Like I said,' the earwig murmured, his eyes starting to spin, 'you ask too many questions.'

As a mountain of frizzy orange hair sprung up from under the earwig's hat, Freya Lemar let out an ear-piercing scream.

'You're not Mr Wig!' she shrieked, pointing at the eye-spinning beast. 'You're . . . You're . . . HYPNO-BUG!'

It was true. Hiding beneath Mr Wig's hat, glasses and big coat was the notorious Hypno-Bug, an ugly earwig who had been imprisoned for years on a remote island in Greenfly Lake. Only now the mad, bad earwig had escaped – with an evil plan up his sleeve. But what was it? And what did it mean for Bugville?

Freya Lemar looked over at Stag, with his vacant expression and Lacey with her glassy stare. Suddenly, everything made sense – they'd been hypnotised!

Freya unbuckled herself and dived at the car door to escape, but . . .

'You're not going anywhere, Miss Lemar,' Hypno-Bug said, locking the door and fixing her with his hypnotic stare.

'Y'see, I'm gonna make Tankie the biggest hero Bugville's ever seen,' he bragged, his eyes spinning with delight. 'Why, that boy's gonna make me super-rich!'

'How?' asked Freya, feeling sleepy.

'Well, first he gonna win me the prize money from Bugville Smash. Then he gonna make me mo' money opening supermarkets, shopping malls, bein' on mo' bad TV shows. Then there's advertisin' sweat pants; magazine deals; releasin' stupid novelty songs and stuff.'

'But what about Superfly and Midge?' Freya yawned. 'They'll –'

'Superfly and Midge!' Hypno-Bug interrupted. 'Why, no one'll wanna be saved by those two losers – ev'ryone'll want Tankie! And then, when my boy's the only hero left in Bugville, I'll make ev'rybody pay to be saved!'

The hideous earwig moved closer. 'And yo' gonna help me make it happen, Freya Lemar. Whether you like it . . . or not!'

Hypno-Bug's eyes swirled and twirled . . . round and round . . . faster and faster. Until, at last, Freya Lemar had been hypnotised!

'Now,' Hypno-Bug sighed. 'T'night yo' gonna tell ev'rybody that Tankie's gonna be the biggest superhero Bugville's ever seen.'

Freya sat, spellbound, on the back seat.

'Got it?' Hypno-Bug asked, putting his hat and glasses back on.

His hypnotised victim nodded.

'Good.' The evil earwig climbed back into the driver's seat and started the car. 'Now let's go.'

The limo sped out of the dirty alley and headed for the TV studios. Then . . .

. . . a giant Goliath beetle burst out
of the shadows – The Tank was ready for
Bugville Smash!

Chapter 13

UP ON THE ROOF

'Why've you dragged me up here?' Superfly grumbled, as he and Midge sat on top of a huge TV screen outside the Fly TV studios. 'We could've watched the final at home with a pizza.'

Midge mimicked his pal moaning.

'And stop trying to look in Bubba's bag!' Superfly snapped, lifting Midge up by the wings.

Midge nipped his finger.

'OW!'

Below them, lit up by fireflies, was the red carpet. TV cameras filmed fans with their banners. Damsel-flies strutted with walkie-talkies. A prancing termite scurried around looking for the limousine. Then, at last, the fans had someone to cheer – Jonathan Moth had arrived.

The show's host posed for photos and chatted, until two familiar Fly Newscasters appeared on the giant screen . . .

Superfly and Midge watched the judges' limo pull up. The crowd pushed forward as a security bug opened the door.

Out climbed Lacey Russell, quickly followed by Stag Taggart. Their fans cheered.

'Phew,' sighed Superfly. 'Stag's OK.'

Midge ground his teeth.

Suddenly the crowd went wild. 'Wow!' cried Superfly. 'It's Freya!'

Midge snarled.

'Hey, cut that out! Freya's our friend, remember?'

But instead, the midge threw back his head and widened his eyes. He thrust two legs out in front of him and started walking like a zombie.

'What's up with you, today?' asked Superfly, shaking his head in dismay. He turned to watch Razorblade as he disappeared inside. But then he noticed someone else crawl out of the limo – Mr Wig!

'Why'd he drive the judges here?' Superfly wondered out loud.

The crowd let out an almighty cheer. The Tank had arrived. But the fans' favourite just stomped inside, without so much as a wave.

'Now that's just rude, ignoring fans like that,' said Superfly. Midge agreed and blew a raspberry in disgust.

'Oh my!' Superfly cried, zooming in on Freya Lemar. 'Look at her big, glassy eyes, Midge.'

The tiny midge slapped his head in frustration. He'd been saying that all along! Superfly never listened to him.

'Freya looks like she's been . . . zombieflied!'

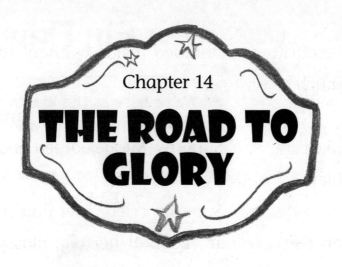

Chapter 14

THE ROAD TO GLORY

Inside the TV studios, Barry Pill, the hilarious millipede, was on stage. Superfly watched the judges suspiciously from the lighting rig. Midge tugged the zip on Bubba's bag, then – TA-DAH! – the show began.

During the break, Superfly pondered the judges' comments. Why did Freya tip The Tank to win when she thought there was something fishy about him? Stag knew some secret about The Tank, but he still said that he would become Bugville's biggest superhero. And if he did, where would that leave Superfly? And Midge? *Midge?*

'Stop that, Midge!'

His pal was spitting everywhere. Superfly scanned the studio below to see who was making Midge mad. It wasn't Melba Modem . . . Or the referee . . . It was . . . Mr Wig!

The suspicious earwig was fumbling in his pocket, but before Superfly could use his 'see-through' vision to investigate, he had to stop Midge drawing attention to them.

Superfly clamped Midge's wings between his fingers and shoved him into Bubba's bag. Then he turned back to continue watching the suspicious Mr Wig.

But Mr Wig had vanished!

As Superfly scanned the studio in search of the earwig, a sudden blast of music welcomed viewers back. The Bugville Smash finalists were ready to rumble.

As Razorblade, the mighty root borer, entered with pompom-waving damsels, everyone stared at the corner opposite.

Stomping to a pumping beat, The Tank burst into the ring and – DING! DING! – the final began.

The Tank pulled a 6-1-9 off the ropes, but Razorblade gave him the slip, jumping up on to the top rope to try and splice The Tank with a scissor kick.

BOING!

Razorblade bounced off the Goliath beetle's chest and smacked down on the ring.

SLAM!

The Tank thumped down on top of him and unleashed the Tank Roll – his famous finisher.

'3-2-1 – you're out!'

The fight was over!

The crowd booed, disappointed that the final had ended so quickly. But one fly was relieved – Superfly. He'd been having a fight of his own trying to keep Midge in Bubba Flea's bag!

Suddenly, Superfly felt a strange

feeling inside himself, just like Bubba had said he would. It was time to look in the bag!

He slipped his hand in and felt something silky. Not Bubba Flea's dirty boxers, Superfly hoped. He felt some kind of mask and then – 'OW!' – a set of sharp teeth. He pulled his hand out, quick!

A tiny bug wearing a blonde wig was clamped to his finger.

'Midge!' Superfly gasped, forgetting his throbbing finger. 'Why are you dressed like that?'

But the midge didn't answer. Instead, he shoved an old, moth-eaten costume in Superfly's face.

'Is this what I think it is? Superfly asked, spreading the costume out wide.

Midge nodded so hard his wig slipped.

'And Bubba Flea wants me to wear it?'

Midge gave him the mask and clapped.

'Then I shall wear it,' Superfly declared. 'With HONOUR.'

Chapter 15
MYSTIFLY

With Razorblade stretchered off, the ring was prepared for the Mayor to present The Tank with the Bugville Smash Belt. But then . . .

Hip-hop beats boomed out, as a masked bug entered the ring. Behind him, his titchy, toothy . . . girlfriend?

Jonathan Moth lifted his microphone. 'WOW!' the host exclaimed. 'I don't believe it! This has got to be the Comeback of the Century! Ladies and gentlemen, welcome back the legendary . . . Mystifly!'

DING! DING! The Tank made an awkward grab for Mystifly, but the nimble challenger tumbled through his legs and sprang up on to the top rope.

The Tank turned and swiped the air, but Mystifly was too fast. He back-flipped off the rope and landed – **SMACK!** – on The Tank's face!

As The Tank staggered blindly round the ring, Mystifly jumped off his head and tripped him up. The Tank slammed face first into the floor. **BAM!**

Mystifly jumped on him and began twisting his leg back. But The Tank didn't yell or cry out in pain. In fact, he showed no expression at all.

Unlike his manager, Mr Wig, who was fumbling in his pocket, pulling an impressive range of angry faces.

What could he be doing? The secret was about to be revealed.

Mystifly's tiny girlfriend flew down into Mr Wig's pocket.

CHOMP! CHOMP! CHOMP! – she loosened the earwig's grip – 'OW-WOW-OW!' – and lifted something out with her teeth. The angry earwig tried to grab it back, but the lady fly hung on, like a dog with a stick.

'Let go!' the earwig ordered, his hat wobbling.

The audience gasped. Not at the ridiculous tug-of-war, but at The Tank!

The champion was up on his feet again, making shapes in the ring.

Shapes like this . . .

and this . . .

and, embarrassingly, this.

Then, suddenly, he collapsed.

The studio fell silent . . . until:

Melba Modem screamed.

Mr Wig became distracted.

The referee turned ruthless.

The judges sat like statues.

The audience grew restless.

And Jonathan Moth entered the ring.

'Let's all stay calm,' he cried. 'Medical attention is on its – OW! What was that?'

Mystifly's girlfriend had poked him in the back with something.

'A remote control?' the host said, taking hold of it. 'What's this for?'

The tiny fly re-enacted the tussle with Mr Wig.

'OK,' said Jonathan Moth, 'so you pulled this remote control out of Mr Wig's pocket . . . won it off him . . . and pressed the "stop" button.'

The fly nodded.

'But what did it stop?'

The toothy bug pointed at the slumped beetle in the corner.

'The Tank!' Jonathan Moth gasped.

The host lifted his microphone. 'Ladies and gentlemen, I've just discovered something truly unbelievable – The Tank is . . . a ROBOT!'

The audience yelped in shock.

'So,' the host continued, putting the remote down on the edge of the ring. 'The Tank is disqualiflied and we have a new Bugville Smash Champion guaranteed a big kiss from his girlfriend . . . MYSTIFLY!'

Chapter 16

MORE REVELATIONS . . .

'Now wait a cotton-pickin' minute here!'
Mr Wig said, snatching Jonathan Moth's
microphone. 'This weed,' he snapped,
pointing at Mystifly, 'is a CHEAT!'
The audience booed.

'He didn't follow the rules!' hollered
Mr Wig. 'He oughtta be disqualiflied!'

'So The Tank being a robot isn't cheating, huh?' A heckling stink bug shouted from the audience.

'My Tankie's not a robot!' Mr Wig roared. 'He's jus' tired . . . The prize money belongs to me – I mean, HIM!'

The audience hissed, but Mr Wig wasn't worried. He hadn't finished yet.

'Who's hidin' behin' that mask anyway?' Mr Wig snarled, pointing at Mystifly.

The new champ said nothing, though his girlfriend wiped off her lipstick.

'I'm talkin' to you, weed!' the earwig growled, prodding Mystifly's chest.

The winner stayed silent, though his girlfriend threw off her wig.

'OK,' Mr Wig sighed. 'Yo' left me no choice . . .'

He ripped off Mystifly's mask to reveal . . .

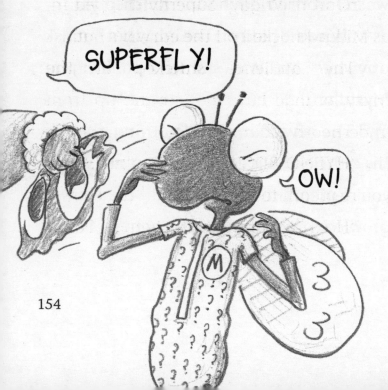

RRRIIIPPP!!

SUPERFLY!

OW!

The audience gasped.

Then the lady fly tore off her dress.

'Oh,' Mr Wig sniggered, 'and Midge –
I mighta known.'

Midge was cross. No one ever took
him seriously. But then, he had forgotten
to take his false eyelashes off.

'Quit it, Wiggy,' Superfly chipped in,
as Midge knocked off the earwig's hat.

The audience shrieked at the
frizzy, orange hair that sprang up from
underneath . . .

'HYPNO-BUG!' Superfly gulped. 'But,
you're meant to be in jail!'

'Hold it right there, Hypno,' Police

Chief De Larentis boomed through a megaphone. 'You're under arrest.'

But Hypno-Bug wasn't giving up that easily! He hadn't escaped jail, built a robot and disguised himself as a wrestling manager for nothing. Why, he was about to make a fortune.

AAAAAGGGHHHH!

Look into my eyes!

Throwing off his dark glasses, he seized a TV camera and stared straight into the lens.

Images of Hypno-Bug's swirly-whirly eyes filled the studio's giant screens, beaming their hypnotic spell to the audience and viewers at home. And once his rich, caramel voice started oozing from the speakers, Jonathan Moth, the pom-pom damsels, the camera crew and the whole audience slipped into a hypnotic trance!

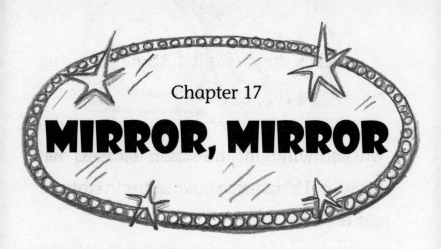

Chapter 17

MIRROR, MIRROR

Well, of course, not everyone was hypnotised.

Let's see: the judges were already hypnotised, so they don't count; the light-headed stick insect on Row 54 wasn't; Grand Master Grasshopper wasn't (but he couldn't see anyway); a booklouse too busy reading a newspaper wasn't;

a sensible midge called Midge wearing sunglasses and ear plugs wasn't; and a drowsy housefly called Superfly (who was searching for a weapon from his belt to stop Hypno-Bug) wasn't hypnotised either.

BLING! A flash of light caught Superfly's eye. It came from somewhere in the audience.

'OW!' Superfly yelped. Midge had nipped him to wake him up. Midge popped a piece of gum into his mouth, then placed some sunglasses on Superfly's nose.

'Thanks, buddy,' Superfly said. 'I forgot I had shades on my belt.'

BLING! The light flashed again.

Using his extra-sensory vision, Superfly searched for the light source.

Front row . . . **BLING!** . . . Seat . . . 68.

He zoomed in. It was Melba Modem's compact mirror that had fallen out of her handbag.

BLING!

Suddenly, Bubba Flea's voice entered Superfly's head: 'Sometime unexpected thing is more use than any weapon on your belt.'

And then Superfly had an idea.

Racing over to Melba's seat, he grabbed the mirror and told Midge his plan.

After a quick high-five, Bugville's heroes flew into action.

With Hypno-Bug glued to the camera lens, Midge hovered overhead, chewing hard. Suddenly, he spat a blob of sticky gum on to the earwig's nose.

SCHLOP!

Quick as a flash, Superfly stuck Melba's mirror into the gooey blob.

'What y'all doin'?' the earwig screeched. 'Get this thing offa me!'

Hypno-Bug tried to yank the mirror off his nose, but the super gum had already set. His hypnotic stare was being reflected back off the mirror. He was hypnotising himself!

Round and round his huge eyes spun . . . faster and faster . . . until Hypno-Bug was hypnotised!

Quick as a flash, Midge grabbed a fold-up chair and whacked it over the bad bug's head.

SMASH!

The earwig slumped back. He was out cold. His hypnotic spell had been broken.

Everyone woke up. The judges: Lacey Russell, Stag Taggart and Freya Lemar . . .

. . . Jonathan Moth . . .

. . . Melba Modem . . .

. . . and, of course, the Police Chief . . .

Chapter 18

WAKE UP

At last, everyone was able to get some air outside, including the Bugville Smash judges.

'So, as he hypnotised me,' Freya began, 'Hypno-Bug told me he planned on getting the prize money from The Tank winning Bugville Smash and then making a fortune out of him doing things like opening supermarkets, advertising sweat-pants and making terrible novelty songs.'

'Oh, that's bad,' Lacey Russell groaned. 'Novelty songs?'

'I know!' Freya went on. 'Hypno-Bug wanted to put Superfly and Midge out of business, so The Tank would be Bugville's only superhero.

He wanted to make everyone pay to be saved!'

Superfly shook his head in disbelief. Midge ground his teeth in disgust.

'So I must've been hypnotised to make The Tank look like he'd be a great hero,' added Lacey. 'Hypno-Bug turned me into a masked villain and made me commit those terrible crimes, so The Tank could stop them and seem like he was saving the day. What a creep!'

'I realised that The Tank was a robot when I watched a replay of the semi finals,' Stag chipped in. 'Y'know I was gonna tell you flies, so that greedy wig-piece hypnotised me to make sure I kept quiet.'

'How could any hero be better than these two?' Freya sighed, smiling at Superfly and Midge.

'Thank you,' she said, gazing into Superfly's eyes. 'Now you'll have to give me that exclusive interview – The Mysterious World of Superfly and Midge: Revealed!'

'Ouch!' Superfly yelped. Midge had nipped him before he agreed to do anything. Midge hated interviews.

Suddenly . . .

The Tank burst through the studio
doors – carrying Melba Modem!

'Look what I found, honey,' Melba called to Freya, waving The Tank's remote control. 'I got a sweetie-pie who's gonna do anythin' I want!'

'Well, at least The Tank's found a good home,' joked Superfly. 'And Hypno-Bug's back on his feet too, look – Wiggy-in-the-middle!'

As news reporters gathered to hear how Superfly had saved the day, the hero felt a dig in the side.

'One moment, flies,' Superfly said. 'What's up, Midge?'

His partner pointed at the crowds. After all that brainwashing, they finally understood something: Superfly and Midge were real heroes, who fought with heart and soul. They might sometimes make a mistake, but never on purpose. They always saved the city because they loved Bugville. And they did it all for free.

Hundreds of expectant eyes stared straight at them. Superfly and Midge were true heroes again. Just like old times.

BOING! Midge twanged Superfly's antennae. A familiar-looking bed bug had squeezed through the crowd to face his idol once more.

'Say it now! Say it now!' the bouncing bug pleaded. 'Pleeeeeeeaaaase!'

Superfly looked round at the watching crowds. They were all waiting for him to say the three words too. Three little words that told them Bugville was safe once again.

'OK, kid . . .' Superfly smiled. 'This one's for you.'

The hero took a deep breath.

He leaned back.

Then he shouted . . .

And so, as the sky lit up with fireworks and Bugville jumped for joy, we can only ask:

Who knew what would happen at the final of Bugville Smash?

Who would've thought a hypnotising earwig would build a robot to make himself rich?

Who would've believed Superfly might nearly give up being a hero?

Who?

Grand Master Grasshopper, that's who.

Woah! It's the Grand Master!
And he's talking to you!

'DANGER!'

Uh-oh! Till next time, bug lovers!

Paul Howard is a very successful illustrator whose illustrations for the picture book of *The Owl Who was Afraid of the Dark* by Jill Tomlinson have been widely acclaimed. Paul lives in Belfast with his wife and three children. *Trouble in Bugville* is the second book Paul has written.

EGMONT PRESS: ETHICAL PUBLISHING

Egmont Press is about turning writers into successful authors and children into passionate readers – producing books that enrich and entertain. As a responsible children's publisher, we go even further, considering the world in which our consumers are growing up.

Safety First
Naturally, all of our books meet legal safety requirements. But we go further than this; every book with play value is tested to the highest standards – if it fails, it's back to the drawing-board.

Made Fairly
We are working to ensure that the workers involved in our supply chain – the people that make our books – are treated with fairness and respect.

Responsible Forestry
We are committed to ensuring all our papers come from environmentally and socially responsible forest sources.

**For more information, please visit our website at
www.egmont.co.uk/ethical**